Fairy World

STELLA A. CALDWELL

BARRON'S

Contents

It is said that only children are able to see fairies—and it was at the age of six that I first became aware of the fairies' magical realm.

It was a summer afternoon, and I was playing in the yard. A soft breeze whispered through the trees, and I gradually became aware that the breeze was in fact a "voice" that seemed to beckon me. It sounds unbelievable, but at that moment I understood that there was more to this world than meets the eye. It was as if a door had opened, and I started to see and hear the presence of fairies everywhere—in flickering movements glimpsed at dusk, in the splash of a still pond, or in the creaks and murmurs of a seemingly empty room.

As the years passed, I started to see more concrete evidence of the fairy realm. I spent countless hours watching for fairy activity, and in time was rewarded by the sight of tiny figures flitting above the flowers of a bluebell wood, or by the spectacle of miniature forms scurrying into an underground burrow.

It is true that children are most likely to glimpse a fairy—for it is they who have the gift to look and listen with believing eyes and ears. But, the world of fairies is open to anyone who truly wants to explore it, and I hope this book— the result of many years of research in far-flung locations, as well as in the woods and skies around my home—will show you that in the fairy world, not all is as it seems.

S. A. Caldwell
Royal Institute for Fairy Research (RIFR)

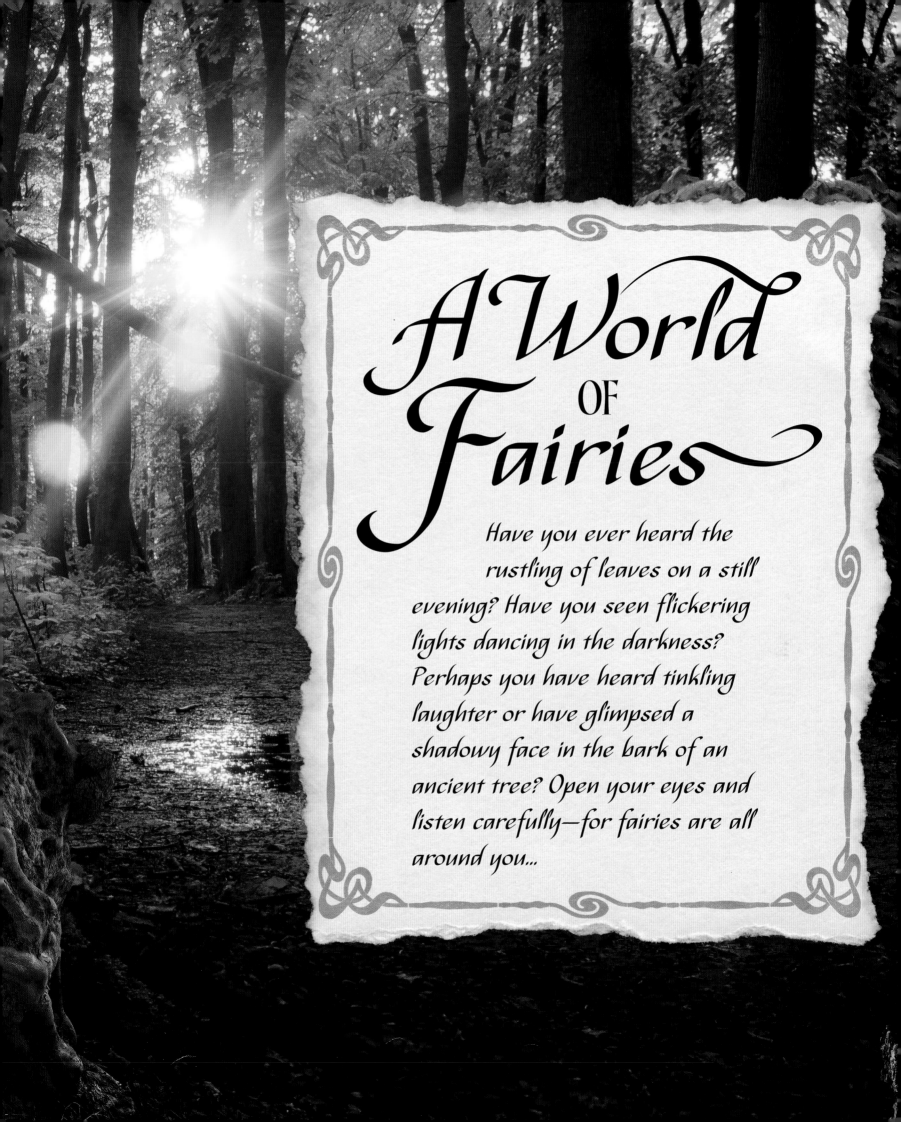

A World
OF
Fairies

Have you ever heard the
rustling of leaves on a still
evening? Have you seen flickering
lights dancing in the darkness?
Perhaps you have heard tinkling
laughter or have glimpsed a
shadowy face in the bark of an
ancient tree? Open your eyes and
listen carefully—for fairies are all
around you...

Finding Fairies

The greatest secret to finding fairies is to believe in them. These elusive sprites are all around us, though most people are blind to their presence. However, if you know where to look and what charms to use, you may just be lucky enough to catch sight of the fairies' enchanted realm.

This feather was dropped by an unusual bird strongly suspected of being a fairy in disguise.

Fairy hunters should always carry a journal to record any unusual signs or possible fairy sightings.

Fairy Signs

The best time to see fairies is at dawn or dusk. Always treat nature with respect and be alert at all times—a flickering movement glimpsed from the corner of your eye could be a darting pixie, or a breeze whispering through the trees might be the murmurings of woodland sprites. Be aware that fairies often travel in disguise—a butterfly or bird may not be what it seems. And if you have ever had the sense of something brushing across your hair, or have heard a soft tinkling music that cannot be explained, then it is quite possible you have already been in the presence of fairies.

Fairies are fascinated by reflected sunlight or moonlight, and a small mirror left out in your yard or near water will almost certainly attract them.

Fairies are guardians of nature, and they delight in all its treasures.

11

Charms and Gifts

* Look for tree hollows, mounds, or tiny holes in the ground. Leave gifts of shiny material, pretty beads, or treats such as honey and cake crumbs.

* Sit next to a pond or stream, and hold out a set of wind chimes to gently summon sprites to the surface.

* Create a fairy garden with flower petals, a tiny pool of water, and gleaming stones and shells. Use twigs and leaves to make a shelter.

* Fairies are attracted to mirrors—leave one out near some flowers and watch to see what happens.

* To protect against bad fairies, always stay alert and carry a charm made of iron.

Fairy Lairs

Fairies make their homes in an amazing variety of places. The curled petals of almost any flower might hide a sleeping sprite, while riverside burrows, hollow trees, a clear water pool, or even a cozy corner in your kitchen all make attractive fairy dwellings. The following "lairs" represent just a small example of fairy habitats.

Smooth rocks and pretty water lilies provide ideal hiding places for freshwater nymphs. These fairies are attracted to shady, peaceful spots where they are soothed by the sound of trickling water or the splash of a waterfall.

Coral gardens beneath the ocean waves provide beautiful habitats for sea nymphs. These fairies delight in dazzling displays of color, and they flit between coral branches like tiny fish.

Sprawling, hollow oak trees provide the perfect lair for woodland sprites. These fairies line their dens with bird feathers or soft moss.

Ancient hillocks and earthworks are home to elves and pixies. If you suspect you have found a "fairy fort," the entrance may be found by circling it three times in a counterclockwise direction while chanting "open door, open door!"

A carpet of bluebells provides the perfect home for flower fairies— the "ringing" of these flowers is said to summon fairies to their midnight gatherings. If you are very patient, you may be rewarded with the sight of tiny figures moving among the bells after sunset.

Almost any bloom might be the dwelling place of a flower fairy. The wings of such sprites usually match their habitat, providing perfect camouflage.

House Fairies

Dark nooks and crannies in kitchens make fitting homes for house fairies.

13

These sprites will often help themselves to household items such as dusters or cotton wool to make their dens more comfortable.

Fairy Features

People often imagine that all fairies are tiny, butterfly-like creatures. However, while some are delicate and dazzling, others are stout and wizened, or even hideous. In the world of fairies, not all is what it seems: Beauty may hide a dark heart, while a beastly appearance may disguise a gentle nature.

Stature

Although most fairies are miniature in size, some species may be much larger. The tiny muryans—meaning "ants"—are indeed no larger than ants. On the other hand, stout dwarfs and elves may reach the size of a human child.

Muryan fairies—as tiny as ants and lighter than air—have sometimes been observed riding on the backs of these insects.

From a distance, dwarfs and elves may be mistaken for small children, but their aged features soon give them away.

Fluttering Wings

Fairy wings are less common than people might imagine, and only a few types possess the gift of flight. Wings may be insect-like in shape and form, and they can be translucent or beautifully patterned. Although they appear extremely delicate, wings are in fact quite robust.

Most flower fairies—like this wild rose sprite—have wings that blend beautifully with the flowers they inhabit.

This extraordinary feather is almost certainly that of a fairy disguised as a bird.

The translucent wings of many air sprites allow them to blend seamlessly with their environment.

Fairy Oddities

Although fairies share many features with humans, they are defined by their differences.

←— ❧ —→

Many species possess long, pointed ears or elongated feet.

The toes of the folletto point backward.

Brownies have flat faces and pinhole nostrils.

Some fairies can take on different forms. For example, the unpleasant hyter sprite may appear as a bird with a shriveled, human-like face.

←— ❧ —→

17

Fairy Finery

❀

Fairies adorn themselves in garments created from the natural world. Bright summer petals or autumnal leaves may be used for all kinds of finery. Bell-shaped flowers, such as snowdrops and foxgloves, are especially popular, as they can be used to create charming hats and beautiful gowns. Pretty accessories, such as jewelry and belts, are made from berries, seeds, coral, and seashells.

❀

Changing Seasons

Making use of vibrant leaves and colorful petals and berries, fairies change their outfits according to the season.

Green is a favorite color, and evergreen plants, such as ivy, are used to make everyday outfits.

Throughout the year, fairies collect colorful berries to create pretty jewelry.

Collected in autumn, acorn shells are lined with thistledown to make charming caps.

The vibrant petals of spring and summer blooms are used to create stunning gowns and matching hats.

The "bells" of snowdrop and foxglove flowers are an essential part of a fairy's wardrobe, and are used to create hats, gloves, and gowns.

Pretty Shells

Water fairies delight in the swirling colors of seashells, which are used to create eye-catching trinkets and accessories.

In human form, selkies wear beautiful necklaces made from glimmering shells.

This tiny shell, icy to the touch, comes from the magical bracelet of an asrai fairy.

Sea fairies decorate their realms with all types of patterned shells.

Feather Finery

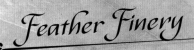

Elves, pixies, and gnomes seek out attractive feathers to add color and interest to their outfits.

A white owl's feather perched on a cap has always been a sign of status among the fairies.

Much sought after, colorful feathers may be stitched together to create stunning dresses.

The Fairy Palette

The color green has long been associated with fairies—for example, the leprechaun never wears anything else but a suit of green. In centuries past, some people believed that wearing this color would attract the fairies' anger, so they avoided it at all costs.

Earth fairies—such as dwarfs and elves—along with many house fairies wear "everyday" working garments in shades of brown or gray.

White is the color of purity—the sidhe fairies, said to give mortals protection and healing, dress in blinding white gowns.

Fairy Trinkets

Fairies delight in pretty accessories, and they are always on the lookout for objects with which to create their trinkets.

This coral necklace, discovered in the ocean depths, is full of powerful fairy magic.

Fairies collect objects discarded by humans—like this piece of string—to create their treasures.

As a symbol of magic and danger, many fairies are attracted to the color scarlet. The sinister redcaps, which inhabit ruined castles, dye their caps red with the blood of their unfortunate victims.

" *Wee folk, good folk,*
Trooping all together;
Green jacket, red cap,
And white owl's feather. "
— William Allingham.

Fairy Kingdoms

From dappled woods to glittering caverns that lie deep beneath the ground, or from tossing seas to the very air around us, fairies inhabit every possible realm. Fairies are rarely seen, though, for the doors to their magical kingdoms are only open to those who truly believe.

Fairies of the Earth

Hairy dwarfs, thickset elves, and squat goblins live beneath mountains and in ancient burial mounds. Some fairies live in hollow earthworks called fairy forts. Legends tell of underground palaces lined with precious stones and of sumptuous banquets held deep beneath the ground.

Precious gems line the walls of the dwarfs' underground caverns and grottoes.

Mountain Dwarfs

When you come across a cave or even a small opening in a rock, be careful! It could lead down to a fairy cavern. Deep beneath the Earth's surface, dwarfs mine for precious stones and metals and live in magnificent glittering halls. These fairies are stout, often very ugly, and have an aged appearance. Daylight turns them to stone, so dwarfs very rarely step above ground. Greedy humans may be tempted to seek out their treasure. Be warned, though— once stolen, fairy gold turns into nothing more than a pile of dusty, old leaves!

The precious stones mined by mountain dwarfs have long tempted greedy humans.

Although dwarfs and elves can see in the dark, many use lanterns to help them with their mining work.

Fairy Feasts

Any human who accepts a drink from a fairy goblet is in grave danger of enchantment.

Walk nine times around a fairy fort on a full moon and you could find yourself a guest at a fairy banquet. In splendid dining halls, fairy folk feast from plates piled high with tempting delicacies and drink from jewel-studded goblets. If you are offered food or wine, however, turn it down at all costs! People who partake in such a feast will instantly see that the delicious food is no more than slugs and snails, and the glittering palace but a dull hole in the ground. Worst of all, though, it is almost impossible for enchanted humans to return to where they came from.

23

Miniature Miners

➤ ❧ ➤

Knockers make their homes in mines and ancient quarries. These tiny workers can be extremely helpful, and the sounds of their tiny pickaxes have been known to lead people to rich pockets of silver and gold. Although largely peaceful, knockers are driven into furious rages by the sound of whistling humans.

The tinny sounds of miniature pickaxes beneath ground are a sure sign that knockers are at work.

CASE STUDY:
Korreds

*I*t was while studying the so-called "dark elves" that I first heard of the korreds. I was visiting Carnac in Brittany, France—a place famous for its ancient standing stones—when I overheard a man describing the elves that were said to live deep beneath the stones. His companion merely laughed, but I knew I must investigate.

The korreds live in burrows deep beneath the standing stones of Carnac.

June 20, Carnac

I have spent the day quizzing the locals. Although some scoffed at the idea of fairies, I saw the look of fear that crossed the faces of many others. Korreds are known for their wild dancing, but as one old man, Mr. Dupont, told me, any human who attempts to join in their merriment will be forced to dance until death. He has offered to accompany me to the stones—I am to bring something made of iron to protect against the elves' magic.

June 25

At dusk, Mr. Dupont guided me to the plain where the huge stones stood eerily silent. Just before midnight, around a hundred tiny hunched figures emerged from the ground. Their faces were half-hidden by shaggy hair, but their red eyes burned through the darkness. When the elves began to dance, they did so with such energy that I felt myself moving to join them. Mr. Dupont pulled me back, and I hastily clutched the iron key I'd brought with me.

VITAL STATISTICS:

Name: Korred

Habitat: Burrows beneath ancient stones

Appearance: Hairy; goat-like hooves; red eyes

Sound: Cackling laughter

Behavior: Hoards precious stones; dances by night

Danger Factor: Bewitched humans are unlikely to be seen again.

Korreds may be identified by their dark, shaggy hair and eyes that glow like rubies.

Scorched Grass

Mr. Dupont and I stayed by the stones till daybreak, whereupon the elves disappeared back into the ground. I felt as if I had been in a trance, the night but a dream. However, when we scanned the site, the grass showed faint scorch marks where the korreds' dancing had burned the ground. And on the ground surrounding the stones, we discovered what looked like miniature hoof prints.

Korreds dance on their cloven, goat-like hooves with such energy that they often burn the grass beneath them.

This blurry photograph is evidence of the korreds' glowing eyes and energetic dancing.

Woodland Fairies

Fairies have long made their homes in ancient woodlands and forests, and legends tell of lost travelers crossing paths with them in these enchanted realms. While some woodland sprites live in hollowed out trees, others make their homes in mossy burrows or among the bluebells that carpet the ground in springtime.

Fairy homes are rarely visible to humans, though at dusk you might be lucky enough to glimpse a magical secret door.

Midsummer's Eve

Fairies are said to dance around ancient oak trees on Midsummer's Eve, a perfect time for the fairy hunter to catch sight of these woodland sprites. Indeed, an old rhyme warns, "Turn your cloak, for fairy folk are in the oak"—it is said that humans can avoid fairy enchantment by wearing their coats turned inside out.

In the summer and early autumn, woodland sprites delight in the sweet berries and fruits that grow in abundance.

The Leshy

While most woodland fairies are well-meaning guardians of nature, the shapeshifting leshy is notorious for tormenting humans. This malicious sprite may appear as large as a tree or as small as a leaf. In human form, leshies have long beards, flowing hair of living grass, and green eyes. Their most sinister trick is the ability to imitate the voices of people familiar to a lone walker. Some lost travelers have been led deep into the woods in the belief that a friend or relative is calling out for them. Unfortunately, only a few have lived to tell the tale, and with only a hazy memory of the experience.

CASE STUDY:
Dryads

Have you ever looked at an old tree trunk and imagined you glimpsed a face in the knotted bark? It is quite possible you saw a tree sprite or dryad, though its face no doubt vanished within seconds. These shy fairies blend in very well with their habitat and for this reason have been seldom studied.

A few years ago, I received the following letter:

I would like to tell you about an ancient oak that stands on a small hill near my home. I believe the tree is perhaps 500 years old, and I have often felt that it is "inhabited." By this I mean that when I walk past it, I sense that something is watching me and on more than one occasion, I have distinctly heard my name whispered above the breeze...

An Ancient Oak

I at once made arrangements to travel to the area, for although the evidence was slight, there is a great need for further investigation of tree sprites. Dryads will object to any human interference so caution is advised. I decided to camp near the sprawling oak, and to make no show of observing it but merely to "blend in" with the environment. After several days, I was disturbed one still night by whispering. At first I thought it must be the wind, and then I made out the following words:

Mortal friend, please leave us be —
You cannot fool a fairy tree.

Mustering all my courage, I peered from my tent and was startled to see a face peering down from the leaves of the ancient oak. The dryad's legs were formed from the great split trunk, and its extended arms were gnarled branches. Then, as I gazed, the vision faded and I saw nothing but a tree against the moonlit sky. I paid heed to the dryad's warning though, and packed my bags that very night.

VITAL STATISTICS:

Name: *Dryad*

Habitat: *Ancient oak, ash, or thorn tree*

Appearance: *"At one" with the tree*

Sound: *Whispers and murmurs*

Behavior: *Shy and secretive*

Danger Factor: *Interfering humans may vanish.*

Field and Flower Fairies

Fairies have always been associated with plants and bountiful harvests. Everything they attend to, from a bank of snowdrops to a field of barley, thrives under their magical touch. Fairies are naturally attracted to beautiful things, and flowers provide them with shelter, clothing, and sweet nectar to drink. Primroses are particularly special to the fairies—some say that humans who eat the pale yellow petals will be allowed a glimpse of fairyland.

Farm Fairies

Meadow elves and pixies often help farmers harvest their crops. They may also watch over farm animals and prevent sheep and cattle from straying. However, they expect favors in return for their hard work, and farmers would be wise to leave out plates of grain and fruits or gifts of warm clothes for their fairy friends. When a fairy receives no gratitude, it may take revenge by hiding farm tools, knotting the manes of horses, or stealing milk from cows.

> " I know a bank whereon the wild thyme blows,
> Where oxlips and the nodding violet grows...
> There sleeps Titania sometimes of the night
> Lull'd in these flowers with dances and delight."
>
> "A Midsummer Night's Dream,"
> - William Shakespeare

Sylphs of the Air

Hidden in wisps of cloud or billowing mists, and carried on the wind, fairies are part of the air around us. Some fairies are guardians of the elements, providing renewing rainfall or refreshing breezes. Other sprites can be more destructive, whipping up violent storms. Air fairies are seldom visible, seamlessly blending with blue skies, mist, rain, and snow.

Windstorm Sprites

Tiny fairies called foletti love to stir up windstorms, riding on the backs of howling gales and shrieking with delight. If you listen carefully, their gleeful laughter can be heard above the noise of a downpour. These fairies sometimes gain entry to peoples' houses by creating a tiny whirlwind to carry them through a keyhole. Once inside, they can carry out all types of mischief, though they are rarely harmful.

The Ice Fairy

The Yuki-onna, a Japanese sylph with a heart of ice, appears on snowy nights. Beautiful and serene-looking, this spirit of the air has flowing black hair and almost translucent skin. However, despite her loveliness, the Yuki-onna's eyes are said to strike terror in the heart of any mortal. Floating above the snow like a mist, this fairy leaves no trace. She may enter homes through open windows and lure victims outside where her breath turns them into icy statues. Other victims may simply be led astray as they struggle to find their way through a snowstorm.

35

The sinister Yuki-onna fairy transforms her victims into icy statues.

Fairy Wings

Throughout my years of travel across the world, I have gathered a unique collection of exquisite fairy wings. From the brightly patterned wings of flower and meadow fairies, to the deep green or blue wings seen on woodland sprites, the rare specimens displayed here demonstrate the dazzling variety found among winged fairies. Although extremely delicate in appearance, fairy wings—like spider silk—are in fact incredibly resilient.

Tree Fairy Wings

Only a very few tree sprites possess wings. The specimens shown here are among the rarest in the fairy realm.

These maplefairy wings were found in the Northeastern U.S.

Featherleaf fairy wings, discovered in Mongolia.

These cherry-blossom fairy wings glow during a full moon.

Woodland Sprite Wings

Sprites found in woodland habitats show an astonishing variety of wing colors.

Of all sprites, the moss fairy's wings are among the loveliest.

These wings are almost certainly those of a stream-dwelling sprite.

The color of a hawthorn fairy's wings changes with the seasons.

These wings are thought to belong to a rare mushroom fairy.

Found in Japan, these wings are those of a pond-dwelling sprite.

These will-o'-the-wisp wings glow a deep red when night falls.

Everlasting Flower

The fairies' magical powers are affected by the flora and fauna that surround them. The everlasting flower is one of their most prized blooms, used for mysterious potions and spells of enchantment.

An everlasting flower that has been touched by a fairy is full of powerful magic.

Flower Fairy Wings

Easily mistaken for butterfly wings, these beautiful specimens have a distinctive glowing appearance.

The wings of the forget-me-not fairy are particularly luminous.

Found in Africa, these wings are those of the everlasting flower fairy.

Green orchids are incredibly rare, and the green-winged fairies that inhabit them rarer still.

Only a delicate fragment remains of this fern fairy's wing.

Water Fairies

From vast oceans to tiny gurgling streams, the world's water regions are watched over by fairy guardians. Beautiful nymphs dance upon the waves, while enchanting sprites flit through lakes, rivers, and springs. While most water fairies are concerned only with guarding the natural world, some have been known to lure boats into dangerous seas and innocent people to a watery end.

Moonlight Nymphs

Incredibly rare, asrai fairies are only ever seen at night when they rise up from the icy depths of northern seas. These nymphs adore bathing in moonlight but must dive back beneath the waves before daybreak, for they cannot survive sunlight. Their beauty is so spellbinding that any human who lays eyes upon one will desire to capture her. However, fairy hunters should never be tempted to steal these nymphs from the sea—it is said that if an asrai touches you just once with her icy fingers, you will never feel warm again.

Legends tell of the fishermen who could not resist capturing a beautiful asrai fairy, who then were doomed to feel cold forever.

Summoning Water Sprites

On the night of a full moon, place a jar half-full with spring water outside, and allow it to soak up moonbeams. Leave it out for two more nights, and then screw the jar tightly shut. When a storm is brewing, place the water jar outside again and allow it to gather raindrops from a thunderstorm. At dusk, take this magical mixture to a place where water fairies are likely to gather—a gurgling stream or a splashing spring. Sitting quietly, sprinkle moonbeam drops over the water's surface and murmur the following words:

Water sprites, I call for thee,
Please take this gift
and come to me!

A jar of glistening moonbeam water combined with raindrops from a thunderstorm is full of fairy magic.

CASE STUDY:
Naiads

few years ago, I spent several months in Greece studying the nymphs that inhabit freshwater springs and streams. These lovely creatures, called naiads, are incredibly timid. Only a few people have ever been lucky enough to encounter one.

July 4, near the village of Sivota
When dusk falls, I sit among the pine trees, quietly watching for the tiniest of clues. I have heard the sighing whispers of tree sprites, but so far nothing that would suggest a naiad.

July 5
Yesterday, I placed a small mirror next to the water and left out tiny portions of melon. There was a faint breeze, so I held tinkling chimes over the water. After a minute, there was a gentle splash and two naiads—exquisitely delicate —appeared. They glanced at me, and my gifts, and then plunged back beneath the surface.

July 11
At around 2 A.M., I heard sweet singing. At first, I could not tell where it was coming from—and then I realized the fruit and mirror had vanished without me even noticing. A few moments later, I saw the shadowy forms of naiads sitting on a rock. They pointed to something that gleamed at the pool's edge—and then slid beneath the water.

All water fairies are attracted by the sweet sound of tinkling wind chimes.

A Precious Gift

I made my way round the edge of the pool to where the small object glistened. It was an exquisite stone, smooth and white. I believe it is a moonstone, much prized by the fairies for its magical properties. Gifts from the fairies are extremely rare and are to be treasured.

Naiads delight in the sweet taste of summer fruits. Leaving some out as a gift is a sign that you are a friend of the fairies.

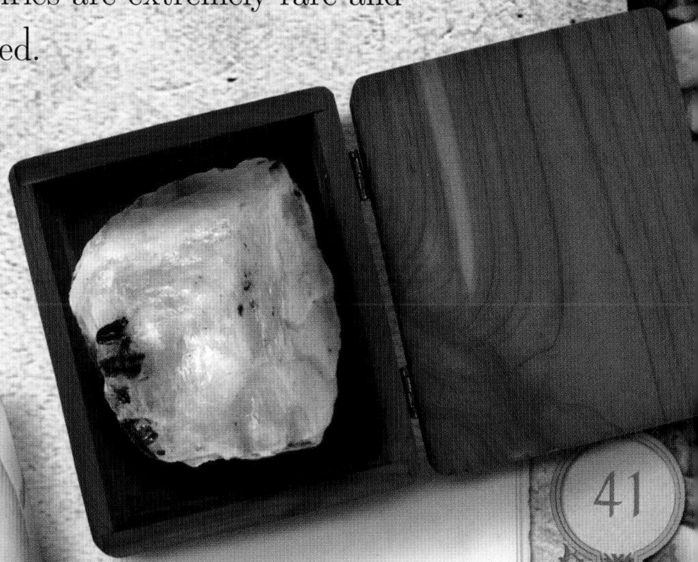

This shimmering moonstone —a gift from the naiads— contains the ancient wisdom of the moon and the stars, and is a powerful lucky charm.

VITAL STATISTICS:

Name: Naiad

Habitat: Streams and springs

Appearance: Delicate; exquisitely beautiful

Sound: Melodic singing

Behavior: Sweet-natured; generous

Danger factor: None, though their shyness may frustrate humans.

Fire Fairies

Sometimes known as will-o'-the-wisps, fire fairies inhabit lonely places far away from towns or cities. They appear as tiny flickering lights that hover above the ground or dart quickly through the air. Some say will-o'-the-wisps will usher lost walkers to safety. However, caution is advised, for legends abound of these fairies leading people far from the security of their paths into boggy land or even to the perilous edge of a cliff.

Enchantment

As darkness falls, fairies emerge from their shadowy realms to sing, dance, and make mischief. Beware, though, for the magic of fairies can be very powerful. Enchanted mortals may discover that the way back to the human world is a difficult one.

The Witching Hour

Fairies are fearful of daylight, and they usually emerge only between the hours of dusk and dawn. The most significant hour for fairies, though, is midnight. This enchanted hour, when witches fly and ghosts creep from the shadows, is when the magic of fairies is at its most powerful.

Fairy Horsemen

Perhaps one of the most frightening yet awe-inspiring sights for any fairy hunter is that of the "wild hunt." As midnight strikes on winter nights, a troop of fairies—accompanied by howling dogs—may be seen galloping across the night sky on ghostly steeds. Humans should remain safely indoors, for it is said that these fairies can suck the souls of the living up into the dark skies. Legend tells that the sight of the wild hunt is a bad omen, foretelling great misfortune— those looking to catch sight of the fairy horsemen must protect themselves by carrying something made of iron or a bunch of rowan berries.

The rowan tree has many protective powers, and a bunch of red berries or a knot of twigs may be carried to ward off the magic of bad fairies.

46

> *"When the winter winds blow and the Yule fires are lit, it is best to stay indoors, safely shut away from the dark paths and the wild heaths. Those who wander out by themselves on the Yule-nights may hear a sudden rustling through the tops of trees—a rustling that can't be the wind, for the rest of the wood is still..."*
>
> — *Kveldulf Gundarsson*

Cockrow

❦

Careless fairies caught out after sunrise will be stranded in the human world until dusk. Many are turned to stone until night falls, when the spell is broken. Humans who chance upon a fairy statue should keep their distance, for touching such a stone can result in a painful "fairy burn."

Magical Doorways

Fairies may enter or leave our world through mysterious "portals." These doorways are often found at wells, springs, or "hag stones"—rocks that have been hollowed by flowing water. Where fairy kingdoms cross paths with our own world, some people have reported hearing strange whispers and laughter, or tinkling music carried on the wind.

Betwixt and Between

Boundaries are often enchanted places where humans may step between worlds. Ancient crossroads are especially magical, as are the shores between sea and land. Sometimes a fairy portal is marked by an unusual rock formation or a twisted tree. At other times, the air may crackle with a strange energy. There are many tales of people who have accidentally stumbled upon a secret doorway and into the fairy realm. Perhaps they crawled through an opening in a rock or unwittingly stepped into a "fairy grove," the enchanted space found between an oak, ash, and hawthorn tree.

Vanished Time

Stepping into the fairy realm is not a matter to be taken lightly, for the normal laws of time do not apply there. Returning humans may feel as if they have been away for a lifetime only to find that time has seemingly stood still. On the other hand, some may feel they have been away for just a few seconds, when, in fact, they have been missing for weeks—or even years.

Fairy Paths

❧

Fairies are believed to travel between their various haunts in straight lines called "fairy paths"—and it is considered very bad luck to build a house on one. You can detect a fairy path by leaving out a pile of stones overnight. If they have been disturbed by morning, then that is a clear sign of the fairies' displeasure.

Fairy Rings

When next you walk through an open field or shady woods, look out for a ring of lush green grass or a circle of mushrooms. These "fairy rings" can be so small you would hardly notice them, though some may grow to be very large. They mark the spots where fairies dance by night and are places of powerful magic—as well as danger.

The Fairy Dance

It is well known that the enchantment of fairy music and joyful laughter can draw passersby to the fairy ring. However, it is always best to observe dancing sprites from a safe distance. Humans that step into the ring can become invisible to mortal eyes, or they may be forced to dance until they collapse.

Enchantment

Stepping into a fairy ring, even by daylight, can bring bad luck. To reverse the spell, run around the ring nine times—though be sure to count carefully! If someone becomes captive in a ring of dancing fairies, you can rescue them by keeping one of your feet firmly outside the ring and reaching in to grab their clothing. Be warned, though—your companion may appear reluctant to return to the human world or may even pull you into the ring.

Magical Trees and Plants

Fairy magic is associated with many trees and plants. Some, like hazel wood or the sacred ash, are said to carry the wisdom of fairies. Other plants, such as daisies or the berries of the rowan tree, may be used to protect against fairy mischief.

Primroses

Place these blooms on your doorstep and fairy blessings will be sprinkled over your home. If you cup a primrose in your palm, or eat the petals, you may catch a glimpse of the fairy realm.

Hawthorn

When covered in white springtime blossoms, "fairy thorn" trees are the perfect place for the fairies' May celebrations. If you break this tree's branches or pick its leaves, however, you risk angering the fairies.

"Hawthorn bloom and elder flowers
Will fill a house with fairy powers."
– Traditional rhyme

Daisies

A daisy chain strung around your wrist or forehead will protect against fairy magic. The flowers are said to resemble the sun, for they open with sunrise and close at dusk.

Four-leaf Clover

Those that stumble across this lucky charm may be granted a wish. Beware of actively looking for a four-leaf clover though, for you may find yourself tricked by a pixie!

Fairy Herbs

Mischievous fairies can bring about annoying ailments such as sneezing or rashes. Herbs such as wild thyme or St. John's Wort protect against these ills, though they should always be gathered on a full moon.

Hazel

Fairies use hazel wood for their wands, for it is said to contain knowledge. Twigs of witch hazel placed around your home will bring good fortune, while a hazel nut wrapped in red cloth and carried in your pocket is a lucky charm.

Elder Tree

A stick made from elder wood offers a lone walker protection from fairy enchantment. Elder blossoms, however, should never be brought into the home, for they will attract malicious sprites.

Shapeshifters

ᵔᏉᎿᏕ

Masters of trickery, many fairies have the ability to alter their form. Some will change into a pretty bird or a butterfly merely to avoid being seen by humans. Other fairies may change their shape for more sinister reasons. For example, the river-dwelling nacken can appear as a pretty white horse at the water's edge—any person who tries to mount its back will be carried down to the river's depths.

Ghastly Guises

Few fairies are more feared than the pooka, for this sprite can take on several terrifying forms. Sometimes it appears as a hideous goblin that demands a share of a farmer's harvest. Farmers who don't agree to the pooka's demands will find their crops ruined. At other times, this sprite takes the form of a black goat with curling horns or a monstrous eagle with razor-sharp talons. The guise in which it most often appears, however, is as a sleek black horse with blazing yellow eyes. Rampaging through the countryside, the pooka horse may seize lone walkers and take them for a truly hair-raising ride.

CASE STUDY:
The Selkie

If you look out to sea at the bobbing head of a seal, you may notice human eyes eerily gazing back at you. Selkies are seals that have the ability to transform into fairy maidens. On Midsummer's Eve, they throw off their magical skins and come ashore to dance. Any selkie that loses its skin, however, will be doomed to remain on land.

A few years ago, I received the following letter from the Scottish island of Orkney:

Some years ago, I did a terrible thing. It was a warm night and, unable to sleep, I went down to the beach. Several seals came ashore and I was astonished to see them transform into young women. I had grown up hearing the Selkie legends and so—on impulse—I took one of their discarded skins and waited to see what would happen. When the women came back, all but one picked up their skins and returned to the sea. The last was distraught, and she disappeared on foot.

When we finally spoke, the man told me he had hidden the sealskin away and had all but forgotten it. However, he had recently heard talk of a mysterious woman who was said to haunt the shoreline at night. He had decided he would leave the sealskin out where he had found it. Having heard of my fairy research, he invited me to watch.

Before the selkie disappeared, she dropped this shell. Listen closely and you can hear the murmur of distant shores...

If a selkie maiden loses her precious sealskin, she can never return to the sea.

June 23, Orkney, Scotland
Last night we hid behind a sand dune. After midnight, a woman appeared in the distance. Her face was shadowed, but as she drew near it became clear she was weeping. Then her gaze fell upon the sealskin—in delight she threw it over her shoulders and before our very eyes seemed to melt away. Seconds later, the sleek head of a seal popped up above the water—it turned for a moment to look at us, and then dived beneath the waves.

59

VITAL STATISTICS:

Name: Selkie

Habitat: Cold northern seas

Appearance: Either a seal or a beautiful maiden

Sound: Sings sweetly

Behavior: Delights in moonlight dancing

Danger Factor: Known to break human hearts

Potions and Charms

Fairies confuse mortals and deceive them with clever spells and charms. The natural world is full of materials that may be added to their potions, from the powerful magic of sunbeams or moon dust, to the healing power of crushed ivy or birch-tree bark.

No human has ever been able to discover the magical ingredients of the fairies' precious ointment.

Fairy Ointment

One of the fairies' most potent substances is fairy ointment. Nobody can be entirely sure what it is made of, though some believe a vital ingredient is the oil of four-leaf clovers. Fairies rub the ointment onto the eyes of their newborn babies, allowing them the gift of second sight. Humans who rub the salve on their own eyes will be given "fairy sight"—magical realms will become clearly visible, and closely guarded fairy secrets may well be discovered. For this reason, fairies will deal harshly with any human who attempts to steal their precious ointment.

Magical Wands

Carved from the wood of hazel, rowan, willow, or ash, wands are powerful instruments of magic. The wood of these trees is said to carry a thousand years of fairy wisdom and can grant the power to see the future. Only the most important fairies carry wands, however, for they may cause terrible harm in the wrong hands.

Carved from the wood of sacred trees, fairy wands are instruments of powerful magic.

Fairy Mist

One of the most dangerous powers at a fairy's disposal is the ability to create a blinding mist. Humans walking in isolated spots, such as boggy marshland or high in the hills, are in danger of finding themselves cloaked in a sudden, thick fog. When the mist lifts, they may find that they have been spirited away to the fairy realm.

Fairy Treasures

Fairies take great pleasure in the bountiful gifts of the natural world. Over the years, I have spent countless long weeks in suspected fairy haunts, patiently waiting for any unusual activity and gathering evidence. The objects displayed here are incredibly rare and were taken at considerable risk. Fairies guard their possessions intensely, and it was necessary to recite charms and leave out special gifts in order to acquire these priceless treasures.

Nature's Wonders

Fairies gather substances from the natural world to create potions and objects of rare and dangerous power.

Spider silk that has been touched by a fairy glistens a luminous white. This "fairy tinsel" is used to create sparkling gowns and capes.

This pot of ointment is now kept locked away, for any human that touches the magical substance is likely to fall under a powerful spell.

Made of hazel wood, this wand grants the user the tree's magical powers of healing and protection.

Riches of the Sea

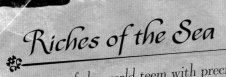

The waters of the world teem with precious treasures, from gleaming corals to the the rare pearls borne from oyster shells.

Water fairies watch over natural pearls—it is said these shimmering treasures contain moonbeams that may grant your heart's desire.

Discovered in the waters of Australia's Coral Sea, this vibrant coral comes from the gardens of a fairy palace.

This Venus comb shell was used by a sea nymph to comb her long locks. If you put it to your ear, you may hear the sweet sound of singing voices.

Gems and Gold

The precious stones and metals of earth fairies have long tempted humans. If you find a hoard, quickly utter the following words before your treasure turns to dust!

Ancient powers of legends old
May I keep this fairy gold?

GREENLAND
Turn this fairy stone over three times to see the future.

STONE FOREST, CHINA
Carry this gem in your pocket, and you will be granted invisibility.

MOUNT ETNA, SICILY
This gleaming stone burns with a strange, volcanic heat.

FAERIE GLEN, SCOTLAND
When held, this stone swiftly changes color from purple to green.

These gold nuggets, from a leprechaun's pot of gold, are the only known specimens of their kind.

The stones above were taken from fairy hoards around the world, and have been found to possess magical powers. They are kept under lock and key, for they could be extremely dangerous in the wrong hands.

Blessings
AND
Curses

Where human and fairy paths cross, fairies may bring sorrow or delight. Although mortals must always guard against malicious sprites, most fairies are fascinated by the human world—and if treated well, may shower us with magical blessings.

Hidden Helpers

airies that move into people's homes can be extremely helpful. Nimble-fingered elves will sew or make shoes for the whole family, while other sprites enjoy sweeping and dusting. Beware of taking a fairy's help for granted though—humans who do not leave out tasty treats may be awoken at night by a clammy hand or find stones in their shoes.

Miniature Housekeepers

Brownies have flat faces and shaggy brown hair, and they wear tattered old clothes. Despite their disheveled appearance, these tiny fairies cannot abide a messy house—while humans sleep, they pick up toys, wash dishes, and have even been known to iron clothes. In return, they expect to be given a bowl of creamy milk and something to satisfy their sweet tooth—fudge is a favorite. Brownies are extremely proud creatures, however. If you tried to give one a new set of clothes, for example, he would be likely to move out immediately.

Industrious elves are well known for their skill as shoemakers. Beware of taking their gifts for granted, though!

The Loyal Domovoi

This hardworking elf can make a household run very smoothly and will always wake the family with loud groans if danger threatens. The domovoi usually makes his lair behind the oven or up in the attic. He is very rarely seen, though unexplained scratching noises or light footsteps may signal his presence. This fairy sheds and renews his wrinkled skin on March 30 every year, and will be very bad-tempered as a result. Always provide extra fairy treats on this day, and make an effort to keep your house spotlessly clean!

67

CASE STUDY:
The Pixie

Pixies are field-dwelling sprites that love to meddle in human affairs. I have studied these fairies for many years, and I have noted that their behavior can be extremely helpful at times—and extremely bothersome at others.

A few years ago, the following newspaper snippet caught my eye:

FARMER'S PIXIE MISERY

BIDEFORD, UK – A local farmer claims his life is being ruined by pixie mischief. Mr. Porterdew says malicious sprites are hiding his tools and pestering his livestock: "I realize people may think I'm crazy, but frankly, I'm beyond caring. Every morning, my horses' manes have been knotted and my pigs are running loose—I've lived in these parts all my life, and I know pixie mischief when I see it!"

Mr. Porterdew says he has yet to glimpse

VITAL STATISTICS:

Name: Pixie

Habitat: Fields and farm buildings

Appearance: Large cheeks; turned up nose

Behavior: Helpful or mischievous; unforgiving

Sound: Manic laughter

Danger Factor: Can be extremely irritating

Knotted horse manes are a classic sign of mischievous farm pixies at work.

September 29, Porterdew Farm

I have been here for several days and have noted several signs of pixie meddling. Mr. Porterdew admits the trouble started after he received the pixies' help in harvesting his crops and failed to acknowledge it. I have advised him to leave out some fairy cakes as a peace offering.

September 30

Last night, I placed Mr. Porterdew's cakes in a corner of the stable and hid behind a hay bale. I knew I was taking a risk, and sure enough, I was startled by a painful pinch on my arm around midnight. I whipped around, and when I turned back the cakes had disappeared. A scrawled note had been left in their place:

> Offend us dear friend,
> and we'll have our fun.
>
> It's too late for "sorry,"
> the damage is done!

Pixie Trouble

I informed Mr. Porterdew that his options seemed limited—offended pixies rarely forgive, and he could either endure their taunts or sell his farm.

Tricksters and Troublemakers

Once a kobold has gained access to your home, it won't leave unless it wants to!

While rarely harmful, some quick-witted fairies delight in playing tricks on humans, and they enjoy the chaos that results when they hide objects or lead people astray. Elves, pixies, and goblins are all known as pranksters.

Tricky Kobolds

If you find a small, damp creature lurking outside your home and you take it inside for warmth, it may turn out to be a kobold. Once this fairy has moved into your house, it won't leave anytime soon. As long as you take good care of a kobold, it can bring you good fortune. However, these fairies are usually more trouble than they're worth—they can't resist playing tricks, and they frequently hide objects or push people over when they bend down, just for the fun of it.

Kobolds usually make unwelcome house guests. They frequently damage furniture and will break items just for the fun of it.

The Hidden Pot of Gold

The fairy's shoemaker, the leprechaun, is almost impossible to outsmart. Greedy humans have long tried to find his famed pot of gold. This green-suited elf makes a promise to reveal his whereabouts, and then—just as the treasure seems to be in reach—vanishes with howls of mocking laughter.

Elf-lock

❦

Elves are well known as talented sewers and shoemakers. However, beware of offending one, for he will take his revenge. If you find your hair is frequently knotted by morning, it could be a clear-cut case of "elf-lock." Leave a peace offering by your bed—perhaps a cookie or a peppermint—and see if the problem resolves.

CASE STUDY:
The Boggart

$\mathcal{I}$t was while studying the unpleasant boggarts that burrow away near bogs and streams that I first encountered a house boggart. I met a woman who told me that one of these squat creatures had seemingly moved into her home. Although he was clearly enjoying the comforts of his new abode, the boggart was proving extremely difficult to live with.

An Unwelcome Guest

Mrs. Elvin told me that she and her family had been living in the house for just a few months when loud noises began to disrupt their sleep. These included slamming doors and the sound of clanging saucepans. Household items had also disappeared—including a favorite soft teddy bear and food—and she had once awoken to see the unsettling form of a goblin sitting on her bed.

Boggarts are extremely unpleasant to look at, and having one in your home may prove to be an unsettling experience.

October 26, the village of Boggarthole

I have been a guest in Mrs. Elvin's home for several days now, and I have had very little sleep due to the racket that starts up around midnight. Last night, the covers were yanked from my bed, and I thought I glimpsed a tiny form scurrying away. I have decided to lay a trap.

October 27

Yesterday evening, I dropped a red silk scarf near my bedroom door—as if by accident—and made an effort to stay awake. At around 3 A.M., I heard a scuffling noise. Peering through the door's hinges, I saw a hairy figure dragging the scarf downstairs. I followed at a distance and observed the creature disappearing beneath the kitchen floorboards.

October 28

When the usual bangs and thumps moved upstairs last night, I realized this was my chance to see the boggart's lair. Creeping down to the kitchen, I lifted a loose floorboard. Beneath was a cozy (if grubby) den made up of a sweater, teddy bears, and a host of other stolen items—including tufts of cotton wool, shiny coins, and my scarf.

Boggarts wear clothing made up of stolen household items. They are particularly attracted by shiny buttons and colorful fabrics, though they favor a "tattered" look.

73

VITAL STATISTICS:

Name: Boggart

Habitat: Dark nooks and crannies

Appearance: Hairy goblin with tattered clothing

Sound: Extremely noisy

Behavior: Disruptive; hoards stolen goods

Danger factor: Will follow a family for life

Fairy Villains

While most fairies are capable of great mischief, a few can be cruel and vindictive. Perhaps the most dangerous fairies of all are those belonging to the Unseelie Court. This troop—consisting of the most hideous and mean-spirited fairies of all—roams the countryside on winter nights looking for human victims to kidnap.

Messengers of Doom

Banshees are dark-cloaked messengers from the underworld. These fairy women usually take the appearance of ugly hags, though they may also appear as beautiful maidens. They always carry a silver comb for their tangled hair—for this reason, it is considered bad luck to pick up a comb found on the ground. Banshees are sometimes seen near water, washing the bloodstained clothes of those who are about to die. However, they more commonly warn of approaching doom by emitting bloodcurdling shrieks and wails.

The fairies that make up the dreaded Unseelie Court are perhaps the most villainous of all.

Banshees are hideously ugly, though they may disguise themselves as pretty, young women if it suits them.

If ever you find a silver comb lying on the ground, you'd be well advised to leave it alone!

Rusalka Nymphs

In the dark months of autumn and winter, rusalka fairies hide away at the bottom of deep lakes. When the days begin to get warmer, these golden-haired nymphs emerge into the sunlight to dance in forests and fields. Humans who catch sight of them are in grave danger of being mesmerized by their beauty. A rusalka will lead her victim to the water's edge, and then down into the lake's icy depths.

The golden-haired beauty of a rusalka fairy hides her dark and malicious nature.

Oatmeal sprinkled over your clothing or carried in your pocket is a powerful protective charm, as is a horseshoe nailed to your front door.

Protective Charms

❖

While it is best to avoid the more unpleasant fairies altogether, fairy hunters must be aware of how to escape their powers. Always carry a protective charm—such as iron, oatmeal, or rowan berries—and safeguard your home by nailing a horseshoe to the door. If bad fairies pursue you, your best means of escape is to leap over water (be it a puddle or a pond).

Meeting the Fairies

Humans have always been fascinated by the fairy realm. It beckons to us as a place beyond the ordinary, a magical world where anything is possible. Fairies are equally fascinated by the human world—tales abound of fairies taking a keen interest in the lives of mortals, or even exchanging their babies for a human child.

Changelings

Legends warn of how fairies—such as the goblin Rumplestiltzkin—are always on the lookout for a human baby to raise as their own. Weary mothers who take their eyes off a newborn infant—even for a moment—may turn back to find that the baby has been spirited away, and a fairy child or "changeling" is left in its place. Telltale signs include constant crying, fairy features (such as elf-like ears), or the ability to speak at just a few months old. Changelings can upset the order of things—family dogs might howl or milk may turn sour. However, it is usually possible for a changeling to become a happy family member and to forget they ever belonged to the fairy folk.

Fairy Godmothers

It is said that every human has a fairy godmother, even if they don't realize it. Wise and loving, this fairy has the power to turn old rags into a shimmering gown and scurrying mice into a team of prancing horses. Be warned, though, that fairy godmothers often "test" people—an old lady who asks for your help to find her missing cat may, in fact, be your fairy godmother in disguise. Only kind mortals deserve fairy blessings!

Keep an eye out for your fairy godmother, for she could appear in your life at any time!

History tells of those children who were spirited away by the fairies, never to be seen again.

Faeries, come take me out
of this dull world,
For I would ride with you upon the wind,
Run on the top of the dishevelled tide,
And dance upon the mountains like a flame.
— W.B. Yeats

Acknowledgments

Throughout my fascinating career as a "fairyologist," I have learned much from those—of ages past and present—who have been blessed with that rare gift of "fairy sight." Their knowledge and wisdom, often gained at the risk of enchantment and sorcery, have always been an inspiration to me.

In addition, I would like to extend my gratitude to those who have made the writing and production of this book possible: my editor, Alex Koken; the designers Drew McGovern and Bruce Marshall; Ryan Forshaw for CGI artwork; Leo Brown for the pencil artworks; Emma Copestake for picture research; and Charlotte Larcombe for production.

Stella A. Caldwell

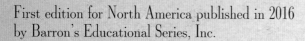

First edition for North America published in 2016 by Barron's Educational Series, Inc.

This is a Carlton book
Text, design, and illustrations copyright © Carlton Books 2016

Published in 2016 by Carlton Books Limited, an imprint of Carlton Publishing Group, 20 Mortimer Street, London, W1T 3JW

All inquiries should be addressed to:
Barron's Educational Series, Inc.
250 Wireless Boulevard
Hauppauge, NY 11788
www.barronseduc.com

ISBN: 978-0-7641-6820-8

Library of Congress Control Number: 2015950116

Date of Manufacture: December 2015
Manufactured by: RRD, Dongguan, China

Printed in China

9 8 7 6 5 4 3 2 1

All images supplied courtesy of Dover Books, freeimages.com, istockphoto.com & Shutterstock.com with the exception of the following.

Key: t = Top, b = Bottom, c = Center, l = Left & r = Right

4-5. © Christie's Images/Corbis, 7bc. Fine Art Photographic Library/Corbis, 24tc. (coin) Mike Fisher/Alamy Stock Photo, 35bl. PhotoAlto/Alamy Stock Photo, 41c. (Nymphaea alba) DK/Getty Images, 59cl. Jason Edwards/Getty Images, 66b. Heritage Image Partnership Ltd/Alamy Stock Photo, 69bc. © Imagebroker/Alamy Stock Photo

Every effort has been made to acknowledge correctly and contact the source and/or copyright holder of each picture and Carlton Books Limited apologizes for any unintentional errors or omissions, which will be corrected in future editions of this book.